THE THUNDERHERD

KATHI APPELT

illustrated by **ELIZABETH SAYLES**

Morrow Junior Books ❧ New York

Pastels were used for the full-color illustrations.
The text type is 18-point Amerigo Medium.

Text copyright © 1996 by Kathi Appelt
Illustrations copyright © 1996 by Elizabeth Sayles

Printed in the United States of America.
1 2 3 4 5 6 7 8 9 10

Library of Congress Cataloging-in-Publication Data
Appelt, Kathi.
The Thunderherd/Kathi Appelt; illustrated by Elizabeth Sayles.
p. cm.
Summary: A lone mustang joins with a wild herd
as it runs down the mountainside to a grassy prairie.
ISBN 0-688-13263-4 (trade)—ISBN 0-688-13264-2 (library)
1. Mustang—Juvenile fiction.   [1. Mustang—Fiction.   2. Horses—Fiction.]
I. Sayles, Elizabeth, ill.   II. Title.   PZ10.3.A68Th 1996   [E]—dc20 95-18198 CIP AC

To Becky and Bill, you of steadfast courage
—K.A.

For Jessica, and all the pretty ponies
—E.S.

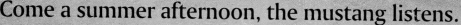

Come a summer afternoon, the mustang listens.

On a summer afternoon, the mustang watches.

This is summer on the prairie, a summer afternoon.
The mustang waits…but not for long…
for high up in the mountains
the Thunder King is gathering up his mares.

Yes, high up in the mountains he's rounding up his herd.
The Thunderherd.

All day long they've grazed in grassy mountain fields,
soaking up the summer sun,
drinking in the melting snow
that runs through mountain meadows.

Now the Thunder King is restless.

He nickers to his silver mares and wispy, prancing foals.

Now the Thunder King is ready.
He leaps above the mountain's peak,
past the startled sun,
urging on his stormy brood
cascading down the mountain.

Below, the mustang braces,
for the Thunderherd is rumbling, rolling,
flashing down the mountain,
filling all the dips and swells of grassy prairie land.

Run, mustang, run!
You of Andalusian heart,
whose grandsires sailed across the sea.

Who carried conquistadores in search of long-lost gold.

Run, mustang, run!
You of sturdy spirit,
whose granddams bore the Blackfoot
across the rolling plains.

Whose kindred drove the cattle north
with cowboys on their backs.

Run, mustang, run!
You of steadfast courage,
sister to the buffalo,
daughter of the wind.

Run to catch the Thunderherd.

Come a summer afternoon, the mustang glistens.

On a summer afternoon, the mustang shines.

This is summer on the prairie, a summer afternoon.